Caliphate Ave.

Leilani Graceffa

Copyright © 2019 Leilani Graceffa

First paperback edition December 2019

Book cover design by Leilani Graceffa

ISBN 978-1-7335558-7-6
ISBN 978-1-7335558-6-9 (hardcover)
ISBN 978-1-7335558-8-3 (ebook)

For more information, visit www.leilanigraceffa.com.

For Christina, those who think they know who these people claim to be, and whom this may concern.

Based on real events.

# Video 1

"Bradley," I hear my little sister utter, placing one of her small hands on my back to shake me awake, "Brad..."

"Yes, Cheryl?" I reply, barely opening my eyes. She opens her other hand in front of me, revealing something mini, about the size of a June bug, in her palm. "Is that a beetle?"

"No," She giggles, "it's a camera."

"Where'd you get it?"

"I found it in the backyard... by the river."

A mini camera makes more sense than a June bug would. There's snow outside. It's still cold to the touch. "You don't want it?"

"No. It's a flash drive, and I don't have a computer for it."

"I'll look in it on my laptop later."

⊙ ⊙ ⊙ ⊙ ⊙ ⊙

A camera... particular for a flash drive. I'll give it back to her if it works. I start to pull on different areas trying to find its USB plug, until I pull apart what is supposed to be the lens part of it, from its body. Even more precise, the USB is the lens part.

I click onto the unnamed hard drive icon as soon as it appears on my laptop's screen.

Expecting it to be unused and have nothing stored on it, I almost remove the plug from my laptop without looking at the window on my screen. But the quick display of a play button beneath the cursor immediately demands my attention. There's not just one play button; there's multiple. "Weird..." I would just disconnect the drive and altogether avoid the fact that I am—could be invading someone's privacy. But a little voice in my head is telling, almost commanding, me to observe further.

So, I slide my finger over my trackpad and click a play button.

I rest my chin in my hand as it begins. But I quickly realize that it's no regular, friendly video when I'm staring at a girl, bound to a chair—with what it looks like her hands behind the seat back—and blindfolded. I know self-bondage is somehow a thing, but she does not appear to have willingly bound herself. I continue to stare at the screen for a least another couple of minutes before I start to hear a couple of voices off-camera getting closer. But almost as if this girl is in a trance-like state, she doesn't budge; her body keeps deathly still.

But it sounds like there are other people there, so it should be fine, and she's just acting... hopefully?

She finally moves her head slightly to the side as the voices eventually subside into one of a guy's, and she hears the sound of a door shutting nearby.

I'll take that back; she doesn't seem to be acting or okay. She's sitting inert like she's suffering from extreme exhaustion.

"Hey, girlie..." The voice utters at her, but she keeps her head in its position, giving him no sort of reply. "We're playing a game." Still, she doesn't move, but she lets out a barely audible groan. He snatches a fistful of her curly hair and yanks her head back—so swiftly that he could break her neck if he did it hard enough—then angles the malicious blade of a kitchen knife at her throat. She's barely conscious enough to even realize what he's doing, but that doesn't stop him. Before removing the blade threatening to gash her throat, he leans into one of her ears, just enough for the camera to be able to see the bottom half of his face, and whispers into it. As I continue to watch this already mad shit, I begin to realize he probably whispered some fucked up thing to her, taking notice of him doing something with his pants... unzipping the fly.

I immediately shut the lid of my laptop before I could witness some other stuff I wouldn't be able to unsee. "What the fuck..." He is not about to rape that girl. Who is this dipshit abusing this girl, and why did he record this shit?

"Bradley," I open my eyes to hearing my girlfriend, Eden's voice behind me, "Are you alright? What's wrong?"

Should I tell her about what I was just watching? I don't want to lie to her, but I also definitely don't want her to be scarred like I already am. "Headache," I answer. Although it's not the direct cause of why I seem agitated, I think one is starting to come. "I'm okay."

"Are you sure?"

"Yeah." I'm fucking glad I didn't let my sister keep this flash drive. After she leaves, I raise my head and then attempt to lift the lid back up, slowly. I don't want to watch this girl get abused at all, but I'm getting the feeling that if I watch enough, I might just see a face, and find out who she and that douchebag is. Fingers crossed.

I lift the lid entirely, after hesitantly gaining the courage to watch more of the video. I have a lot more to go too, so I might as well get used to it now.

⊙ ⊙ ⊙ ⊙ ⊙ ⊙

It makes me want to smash my laptop and the flash drive knowing that I can't help this girl, it could still be happening to her, or in the worst-case scenario, she's dead, and there's nothing that can be done. I have a little sister, a girlfriend, a mother, little cousins, knowing that there's disgusting, fucked up people out there like this guy who would do this kind of shit to any of them, to anybody, and fucking record it, fucking crushes my soul.

She doesn't even look that old either! She looks like a damn teenager! Teenager or woman, this guy needs to get his ass beat by her family, then get thrown under a prison!

"Bradley!" I hear Cheryl's call close. Before she comes into the room, I quickly wipe away tears from my eyes. Not even concerned about the flash drive, like I expected her to be, she comes to tell me, "There's food downstairs."

"Okay. Thanks, Cheryl." Maybe talking to Eden and Cheryl will take my mind off of this. I know it will be back. But before heading down there, I remove the damned flash drive from the USB port. I'm not sure when's the next time I'll be ready to view the rest of the videos.

"What's wrong, babe?" Eden instantly notices my puffy eyes... and I guess how upset and agitated I still look. But I don't want to—can't—tell her why, and I fucking hate it.

I can't use my previous excuse. "Movie," I answer.

⊙ ⊙ ⊙ ⊙ ⊙ ⊙

I'm still at a loss for even a word. I haven't finished watching the entire video, I don't want to, and I'm not going to. So, I just sit in front of my computer covering my face, still trying to process what I just witnessed, and trying to gain the courage to click onto something else. Apparently, there are not only videos, but there are photos as well. And as much as I wish I didn't know that so I wouldn't be even more curious, I know now, and for some reason, I'm still interested in looking at a photo. Just one.

Jesus Christ. I remove my hands from my face and move the pointer over the nearest file without a play button over it. I can already see it's not a pleasant looking one.

I think it's the same girl, arms and legs tied behind her back with ropes, lying fetal position on the floor. With no way to see her face due to her hair covering it. There's no way she's willingly doing any of this and wanting pictures taken of her like this. Whoever snapped the picture and recorded the video—in which it has to be the same guy in the video—needs his ass beat and hung by his balls immediately.

Photo 1

"Bradley!" Cheryl immediately sprints towards me as soon as I walk into the door. She hadn't done that since she was a baby, ecstatic to see me when I got home from school every afternoon, so she must be excited about something. "Can you take me to see Austin?" She asks.

Who? "Who is Austin?"

"Bianchi."

Oh, that Austin, the one Eden used to like and religiously listen to. She doesn't anymore, suddenly. It's been a while. "Did you ask mom or dad first?"

"They said I can go."

Before I reply to her answer, I look up to notice Eden, sitting at the kitchen table, probably doing homework, and halfway listening in to us with an awkward expression on her face. "Is it a concert, or...?"

Then Eden finally adds on with, "He's doing a tour. He'll be in Atlanta next Wednesday and Jacksonville on Thursday. I told her to ask you before buying a ticket. If you choose Atlanta, you'll take her, Jacksonville, I'll take her."

"Okay, I'll take her. Why do you have that look on your face?"

She hesitates before lowering her head. "I'll tell you later."

"Do you still have that flash drive?"

Fuck, fuck, fuck, fuck. I knew my sister would ask about it sooner or later. I haven't touched or even thought about that thing in days. Now that she's mentioned it, it's back in my headspace. I have to lie to her about it too. "Uhh..." Tongue-tied, I try to think of a quick answer to her, "I haven't checked it yet."

⊙ ⊙ ⊙ ⊙ ⊙ ⊙

I haven't even dug deeper into the drive yet, and it already makes me nauseous seeing it and having it in my hands. I hate it. But I need it, and I have to dive deeper if I want to find out who owns it and why the contents of it are heinous.

So, instead of clicking on another video, I scroll a few notches further into the drive. A slightly light leaked picture of a girl with long curly hair, the same girl I presume, with her arms appearing bounded behind her back. But most of her face is hidden behind her hair as she's looking down, either at the ground, at her knees, or at the noticeable puddle of... looks like vomit in front of her. She's not in a chair; she's on her knees, with absolutely nothing on. Luckily, by the angle her head is in, her hair covers almost everything.

Whenever I find and get a hold of whoever is responsible for this, I'll beat his ass first before handing him over to the authorities and let them let her family hand his ass to him.

Now, for this next video I have to watch, she appears to be pretty conscious and functioning correctly, but she's still wearing a blindfold and something that wasn't there before, a black choker that looks a lot like a dog collar around her neck with a chain attached to its ring. I don't get why she can't just get up and get out unless she's not as conscious as she appears, or something the camera can't see is binding her from getting up.

I can only assume the chain is binding her to something, like a fucking dog.

She's only able to move her head... and now I know why. I hate to describe or say any of what I'm seeing. He bounded her down to keep her from moving around and trying to pull away while he's forcing himself down her throat, and I'm sure to do some other fucked up shit too.

My head is starting to throb just wanting to ask, "Why? Just fucking why?"

Video 2

I'm not sure how I'm still able to get an acceptable amount of sleep after the shit I've been witnessing this week. Juggling college classes is one thing, being the unexpected detective of a crime is a whole other world. I know nobody is forcing me to investigate it, but I'm sure you get the point already.

For today's gruesome sighting, the girl is lying a few feet away from the camera, naked and blindfolded, and obviously dazed and barely conscious even though it looks like she's slowly trying to move her body. If she weren't in a hypnotic state, she would be thrashing around trying to escape. Someone else is in the room with her.

I probably shouldn't be eating while watching this because I know this guy is going to do something unforgivingly fucked up to her. It's entirely on me if I end up vomiting and possibly ruining my laptop. So, in preparation for whatever I'm about to witness, I immediately set my food aside and push my computer further away from me, almost to the other end of the table. She's so numb that she doesn't even flinch when the needle of a syringe penetrates her skin. Is he trying to keep her almost blacked out unconscious, or can he somehow tell the previous supply is starting to wear off? She's utterly, and scarily, oblivious to him standing over her. Not only is he holding a syringe in one hand, but he also has a fucking camera in the other; I'm guessing the same one he used to take the other pictures on here. Taking fucking photos of her in that state. Why the fuck...?!

This sick motherfucker. I can't. I can't watch this. I see this girl as another person I genuinely care about, even though I don't know her, and she's never seen me a second in her life before. Seeing her being treated as ungodly and inhumane as possible shatters my heart and makes me want to keep all the girls I know and pretty much every vulnerable person in a jar where nobody can hurt them. But unfortunately, that will never be possible. Shit like this will always be happening to someone as long as the main gates of Hell stay wide fucking open, letting out the most unworthy pieces of shit nobody would care about if they vanished off the face of the Earth right now. He's one of them. And I wish this motherfucker would show his face so this shit can be over with, and he can get everything coming his way when he gets convicted and thrown under a prison with other people like him!

Eden is not going to be happy if I throw away this food because my stomach is no longer fit to eat the rest anymore.

⊙ ⊙ ⊙ ⊙ ⊙ ⊙

Here it is, not being able to sleep. Luckily, I have my last class of the week in six hours, but it doesn't help to know. I guess it's time to distract myself until my eyes get heavy. My laptop is calling me, which means I'm not getting a second of sleep tonight. So, like the hard-ass head that I will always be, instead of continuing to try to get the rest that I know will never come, I get up and take my laptop downstairs with me; at two in the morning. Why am I even torturing myself? I'm not watching a video this time. I'm already a step from turning in this drive to the police for them to investigate themselves. Then they probably won't do anything because they can't figure out who owns it, or just come after me because I'm the last person who had it. I don't need another unjust investigation done on me, not after that murder trial.

I begin to swipe through the drive once again. Searching for a less gruesome photo to examine... if one even exists out of all the other ones. Until I eventually do come across one just a bit, I said just a bit, less gruesome than the ones I've already seen.

The girl is still unconscious, lying head down near someone's feet. It doesn't sound as bad as it looks. But at least she isn't naked in this one, and I have a little bit more to work with to be able to identify. On the left side of the photo, a hand is in the shot. I know that could be anybody's hand, but not with a distinct and honestly, cool-looking black ring on it. Not sure if it's a custom engagement or wedding ring—hopefully not—or it's just a regular custom one.

I'm barely able to make out its design. And the more I try to get a clear view of it, the harder it gets. It has a black, shimmering stone on it, and the entire band is black. Not a very pictorial description, but I can save the picture on my phone to use for further investigation.

Poor girl. I hope she's still holding on tightly and nothing worse happened to her.

Photo 2

These photos are getting more and more disturbing the further I look. And I still haven't been able to catch one face. The guy is smart, unfortunately. At least I have the ring, and I will continue to look for it in other pictures to be able to make out the rest of its design. And Eden is starting to notice "my energy is off," and that I'm beginning to look like I haven't had a good night sleep in almost a month, so I must be doing this entire investigating thing right.

"You're not acting like yourself, Bradley. You've been down all week." She says. "What's wrong?"

"School," I try to smile, "I'm just stressed."

"I've seen you stressed many times, you've never slowed down, not like this."

"Okay... have you ever... cared about someone you don't know; they have no idea who you are, and you want to help them, but there's this invisible wall between you and them? You're watching them get hurt, and you know you can't do anything."

"Yes."

"That's how I'm feeling now."

Thankfully, not knowing exactly what I mean and what I'm talking about, she replies with, "I mean, there's not much you can do, but standby, and maybe be there afterwards. I know it's not a fun position to be in. Is it a friend?"

I nod. "Yeah."

"Give it time, then tell me how it goes." She smiles.

⊙ ⊙ ⊙ ⊙ ⊙ ⊙

This photo doesn't seem that bad at all; it's the fact that she's being forced to do this stuff. I can't tell if she's blindfolded or not, her head is turned aside as she's sitting on the side of one of her legs below someone and seems to be getting pulled up by a hand that's wrapped around one of her wrists.

It's a bit hard to explain, but it looks like the kind of photo that would be the cover of an erotica novel... of course, if this girl wasn't underage. Is she naked? Certainly. Let's see what will happen in this next video.

It looks like either before or after taking the photo. For once, the girl is fully conscious and trying to move her body around. Attempting to get away from this guy. But she can't get anywhere because he's holding her down across his lap. Somehow, I know he has a smile on his face, even though I can't see his face, knowing damn well what he's doing is fucked up and for some reason, hearing and watching her sob and struggle turns him on. Sadistic motherfucker. As he's holding her down with one arm, he's caressing her butt with his other hand.

It also seems like somethings preventing her from screaming out loud. Something was put over or in her mouth to avoid it. Otherwise, she would've been started raising hell. I really can't help but feel for this girl. And I bet nobody else knows about this, but me for now, most likely because she's afraid to come out about it, and he scared her into being quiet. "Connie..." He murmurs before pulling her back onto her stomach.

So, her name is, might be, Connie? Noting that. I'm starting to get to that point where I don't want to watch anymore. Just watching him assert dominance onto this poor girl fucking irks me.

Carrying on, she continues to try to jerk and twist her body around to fight his grip, even though she already has the idea that it's not going to work. I guess it doesn't hurt to try. But she eventually gives up.

I can't watch anymore of this, but at least I got another handy clue.

Video 3

I plan on telling and showing Eden all of this eventually. I feel I'm close to finally uncovering who these people are. Even though I don't have much evidence yet, I can still feel it. I have to hurry up before I take my sister back home later this week because I know she'll be asking for the drive again. But I could always buy another one and transfer all the photos and videos from that one. I might do that... or purchase a new one that looks like the one I have, to give to her. There's no way in hell I'll be giving this one to her.

Anyway, this video. It doesn't look like it'll be like the others, but one still shot can deceive the entire content of a video. Let's see. It seems like the camera is set on something nearby Connie's, or someone's bed, in a bedroom. Maybe on a dresser or a small table? I don't know, but it's tall enough to see Connie doing something to her hair while staring into the mirrored wall on the farthest side of the room, and she doesn't seem to notice the camera behind her. Finally, something not insane, I think. I hope I didn't speak too soon. Wait, why is she being recorded then? Never mind, I did say it too soon.

It looks like she's using a flat iron to straighten her hair. But enough of trying to figure out what she's doing. While she's doing what she's doing, a guy quickly walks in and places a glass full of water onto the nightstand next to her bed, then sets a plate full of food near her. I hope this isn't the same guy, doesn't seem like it. She suddenly gets a little startled by his presence after looking up from something, probably her phone. This is a different guy. She got startled but didn't jerk or run away.

"Are you alright?" He asks before patting her on the head.

"Yeah." She replies, rather quickly.

He must know about everything happening to her. If not, he's witnessed all of her drastic changes and how exhausted she is. He doesn't leave immediately; he sits on the bed next to her, offering to straighten the reminder of curls on the back of her head. That's sweet. But the quiet moment doesn't last for long. As he is getting the last of them, a familiar voice is heard off-camera. "Ansel..." They exchange a couple of sentences between each other before the first guy finishes straightening the last of Connie's hair, and then quickly leaves the room.

The animosity between this guy and Connie. Even though everything is quiet for now and I can't see her face, I can tell she's sulking. Who can blame her, though? The guy's a useless piece of shit. And so, I bet, to grind her gears and piss her off even more, he starts snapping at the girl upon noticing a scowl on her face. "What is wrong with you, Connie?"

"Nothing! Why do you fucking care?!" She lashes out, "Get the fuck out of my room! Leave me alone!"

She is not in a pleasant mood at all. The man starts fuming. Snatching her by her newly straightened hair, getting in her face, and snarling, "You... don't get to talk to me like that!"

He abuses the child, then expects her to give the same respect he never gives her? This guy needs to go fuck himself. I hope she scratches his entire fucking face off. Dickhead. Not too much shit has happened yet, and I'm already sick of him and this video.

Moving on to a photo... and this next photo, again, it's not as bad as some of the others, but it's still creepy as fuck and doesn't need to exist. It's another light leaked photo. It's a picture of Connie sleeping on one of those corner couches. Or at least it looks like she is, and she's not drugged.

But she's wearing a dress, and there's a clear view of what's under there. So now, I wonder if this was taken solely of her or her and for the undershot. That is so fucking insidious.

Photo 3

I searched online for a flash drive that looks like the one I have, last night. It was an easy search and purchase, thank God. I'll give it to Cheryl whenever.

This is the last time I'm opening this flash drive for the week. If I don't find any other sort of clue after these, then so be it, I can wait. The problem is, Connie can't wait. And the more time I take, the more danger she's in. So, I'm keeping my hopes up for these next two.

So, this next and last photo for now, whoever this asshole is abusing Connie, he's in it. I can tell by the hair. Curly-haired girl sitting next to him... or in his lap, disturbed to even mention that, is Connie. Still unable to identify either of their faces with black scratch markings over the top half of their faces. He appears to be kissing her on the cheek, holding a glass bottle, either a beer or soda, in one of his hands. She doesn't seem to be uncomfortable, if anything, she's almost smiling, while also holding a glass bottle in one of her hands.

This photo isn't all that disturbing if you don't think about it. You'd immediately think it's just two young adults having fun. That is until you realize, Connie most likely isn't an adult, and she's around him, drinking alcohol. I also see the black ring on his finger again, can't make out its design here either, it's not turned the right way for me to do so.

You already know how I feel about this.

"Bradley." I hear Eden call from across the table, her voice sounding a bit more stern than usual. Something's wrong.

I lower the screen of my laptop from in front of my face. "Hm?"

"You're still going to take Cheryl to see...?"

"Sure." I almost figured it would be better for Eden to take her since she's been to one of Austin's concerts before, but she has her classes in the afternoon. The gig is late in the afternoon.

She shrugs before saying, "Oh, okay..." in kind of a tense way. Now her energy is or seems off.

So, before she gets up to leave, I quickly ask her, "Why?"

She instantly sits back down into the chair. "It's nothing serious, but I don't like Austin, and I'm worried about your sister since she's also an empath. You probably won't understand this."

"I'll try. What do you mean?"

"Honestly, I don't know yet. When I went to go meet Austin years ago, I went from happy to wanting to run the fuck out of the room. I don't know if it was just me being nervous, or something is really wrong with him, but that energy that overcame me was very nasty. Whenever y'all come back, I want you and Cheryl to tell me if you felt the same, and it's really him, or it's nothing."

I remember her going there because it was shortly after we started dating. "That's why you suddenly stopped being a fan?"

"I stopped listening to him because he's creepy. He tried to get too close to me, and he was asking the strangest questions."

The guy is a creep, noted. I'm sure he doesn't do the same to his younger fans, hopefully. So, Cheryl should be okay. Otherwise, if not and he's a pedophile too, I'm beating his ass and reporting him if he's even a tad bit creepy towards my sister and other people. "Did he touch you?"

"No. I would've been stood on his neck if he did."

Then that gross energy she felt was most likely his, and it was damn correct and trying to tell her to get away from him. "Okay, thank you for telling me that. I'll watch out for anything." It's tomorrow afternoon, and now that I know all of this, I'm not ready to face this guy if something happens.

Onto this last video, I'll try to watch the entire thing. Again, this one doesn't look like it's going to be that bad. But I don't want to talk too soon like before.

Connie is blindfolded again; the same guy is sitting close to her, and the room is scarily quiet. Just as I think this video isn't going to be as bad as the others, he starts going in on Connie. And I don't mean just straightforward French kissing her, having one of his hands between her legs and everything that shouldn't be fucking happening between them. The scary thing is, it's like they've done this shit many times before. She doesn't seem to be a slight bit uncomfortable by what he's doing to her at all.

Another thing, you'd think this shit is softcore porn when you don't think about it. I'm 100% sure as hell of the fact that he's an adult and Connie is a minor. You know what I'm trying to say and what I mean. But never mind, I take back trying to watch this entire video since I now know what it consists of.

 *Video 4*

Oh, I forgot, Austin is a world-renowned celebrity, and celebrities rarely ever face the well-deserved consequences for any shitty thing they do. Because there's probably plenty of other women who know he's a creep and they're afraid to speak up about him. Let's hope this fucker has enough common sense in his head now to not try that shit today or any other day.

Now I know I'm probably doing one of the devil's deeds taking Cheryl to see this guy, but I can't say no to my little sister wanting to meet him, and she most likely wouldn't understand why he's not as sweet and innocent as he makes himself out to be.

⊙ ⊙ ⊙ ⊙ ⊙ ⊙

Keep in mind that I've never even seen this guy before; I've only heard his voice, so I don't know who is who on the stage. I assume he's not out yet. So, eventually, after a short minute wait, a tall, pale guy with semi-long dark brown hair and a black tank top on, yes, in this cold ass weather, comes out. It's Austin, and I'm now hoping my sister is only here for the music and not for anything else because everybody else here seems to be in their late teens, early and late 20s. I probably should've asked Eden more about this first; nothing said this would potentially be for adults.

If I've ever seen a crowd go insane for a less eerie appearing version of a famous DJ—without half of his hair shaved off—, it's this one.

Anyway, he smiles, then lets out a barely audible chuckle, "Hello!"

One thing nobody can debunk is that he actually has talent, he's a great artist. It's just him as a person. It always seems to be troubled people with all the skills and abilities. But of course, he doesn't show that side of himself... or people know and don't take it seriously.

"Ready for the last one?" He asks.

Last what? I hope it's not his last song.

Just so my sister wouldn't be stuck in the middle of tall heights, not being able to see due to her short height, I kneel and let her get onto my back. When I tell you that, he suddenly starts singing in this demon with a wicked and scratchy, sore throat voice attempting to channel the most compelling demons from the lowest tiers of hell that immediately offends and almost splits my eardrums... you already know where I'm going with this. I expected something totally different. I don't mean to offend the guy at all, but I don't listen to enough rock and metal for this to be easy on my ears. But if Cheryl likes it, then I guess I'm down for it, just for today. I've only heard his lighter and smoother vocals songs that Eden listened to, an entirely different genre. Who the hell trained this guy and how does he have such a broad vocal range?

So, after three or even four minutes of this song causing rooted strain on everybody's eardrums from the strident beat, the entire sound of the venue reduces almost to a halt. I'm honestly scared of what he's about to do next.

My worst nightmare. This guy takes off his tank top. Of course, you're probably asking how is that bad? I have a seven-year-old kid with me, and I'm sure there are many other kids here too. Even though she's my little sister, I would never let her see me, or any grown ass man shirtless until she's well old enough. So what makes you think a random guy is gonna be any more acceptable? And again, I never saw any form of age restrictions while purchasing tickets, so he's doing this in front of minors!

Here come the more soft-toned songs I was talking about, but it's the promiscuous ones. Now, before I get in trouble for letting my sister hear this, I quickly make her get off of my back, then cover her ears. She understands. I'm not sure who this guy thinks he is with this shit, but he better start enforcing some kind of age restriction for future gigs before he gets the right people or parents. In fact, he did get the right one today. I'll let Cheryl hear this part of the gig, inappropriate for her age, be a fan or whatever, but I'm filming it for the useful reference that Eden is right about this guy being a creep.

Photo 4

I don't feel any negative energy yet. I said yet... if Austin comes back out and Cheryl or I suddenly feel some nasty energy overcome us, like Eden said she did, it's definitely him. But I'll watch Cheryl closely and see if she immediately has an awkward expression upon her face near him.

She's most likely going to hate me for this when she's older and learns how sick this guy is.

Meanwhile, I have my head down, texting Eden about the whole thing and the video I took, while blindly feeling and following where my sister is going. And as I'm holding onto one of her hands, she gives me a mini heart attack when she suddenly and quickly wiggles her way out of my grip. Who's fucking jaw do I have to break?! "Cheryl!"

"Hey, kiddo!" I hear a voice chuckle, then my sister's laugh before looking ahead. Austin, holding Cheryl. Not sure if she ran to him or he grabbed her, either way, I was a tiny moment from taking her back and caving his face in. Also, I still don't feel any negative vibe... I don't think. And I guess she doesn't either since she appears ecstatic.

It's actually cute, of course, when you don't think about it and how he is as a person. I'm thinking about it now, it's not so cute anymore. Anyway, I quickly snap a picture of them, he finally puts Cheryl down after taking a minute to talk to her. When she gets back to me, the instinct I didn't realize was bugging me while watching him until now, eventually starts to gradually ease off as we walk away from him. I'm not trying to say something really is up with Austin, but... he's strange. And the fact that he picked her up like she's a baby and unable to stand up next to him on her own... I don't fucking know anymore.

I can't exactly claim him as what's currently in my mind, but Eden's right. He's fucking strange. I had a gut feeling, but if Cheryl didn't seem to mind him like Eden said—her being an empath, she most likely would—I don't know what to think. Maybe I'm overreacting. I can analyze and dissect what just happened for the rest of the day, but I'm not about to do that now, not until I get back to Eden and tell her everything.

⊙ ⊙ ⊙ ⊙ ⊙ ⊙

Last place of the day, the pop-up shop. Specifically for Cheryl, but if I find something that I like, I'll get it.

It doesn't take Cheryl long to pick out what she wants. She never asks for much, anyway. But for myself, I'm stuck trying to choose between three unique appearing rings: different coloured plates—silver, black, and dark blue. I could just buy all three, but I don't want or even need that many rings. I pick the dark blue one. So, we bring our handful of items to a nearby counter where two girls behind it are having a conversation from different sides. The one the furthest away with the long, dark auburn hair and olive skin seems to be more into her phone than the convo, and she doesn't notice us, so the other one with the long, jet-black hair, pale skin, and kind of scary black eyeshadow on takes us.

So, while this girl is scanning everything, my eyes proceed to keep wandering back to the girl with her nose all in her phone, nothing wrong with her, just wondering what's got her full attention.

# Video 5

"He's strange, Eden." I try not to say loud enough for Cheryl to hear. "I didn't feel anything at first, but when he picked Cheryl up like he didn't just see her standing on her own... my gut went crazy." I can't just be overreacting. Otherwise, who else would pick up and hold a random person's child like that?

"Did Cheryl do or say anything?"

"She was completely oblivious." All I can consider now is that I'm not bringing her to any of those ever again. Hopefully, Cheryl doesn't become more of a fan and end up wanting to go to more of his events, and eventually finds out and understands how messed up he really is because that's not happening again.

"Well, if you felt something, then it wasn't just me. Something really is wrong with him. I'm sure other people think so, but they brush it off and continue to let their kids near him."

And that is another thing I don't, and probably never will understand. Maybe some are unsure like she was, but the ones who are sure of the vibe he gives off and continues to attend his gigs, they must not give a fuck about it and give him any fucking pass because of his status.

⊙ ⊙ ⊙ ⊙ ⊙ ⊙

"Cheryl," I call out before closing the lid of my laptop, "turn the tv off when you're done." It's late, she's usually already in bed around this time. No answer. "Cheryl?" I get up, walk into the living room, and look over the couch to find her sound asleep, with her iPad next to her head. She must've been controlling the tv with it. She left a video playing. It's Austin... again. I'm honestly sick of this guy after today, but I've also never seen a video of his. So, I grab the remote from the other side of the couch, and while holding it in my hand ready to switch the tv off, I stand watching the remaining minutes of the video of this guy just talking about random shit while walking around with the camera on him.

Is this what people do nowadays, talk to a camera and make money talking about random things? I shake my head. At least this isn't the only thing he does.

Anyway, as I'm ready to press the power button on the remote, something that moves in the vicinity behind him captures my eyes. And it catches my attention because it looks like a dark, strange figure walking past the white wall at first... but as I go up to get a closer look after rewinding, then pausing it, I'm able to make out the back of someone with long, dark curly hair, leaving the room. But that's not all. I press the play button, wait until the last couple of minutes of the video to replay, and while he's talking and moving his other arm around, I notice something on one of his fingers. A black ring, one of those rings I saw at the pop-up shop. I rewind it again, this time, pausing it the moment this person in the background appears, the side of their face and body swiftly in the frame, it's a girl. Long curly hair and brown skin.

You gotta be fucking kidding me.

Leaving the tv paused, I put down the remote, go upstairs to grab the flash drive, then go back downstairs to open my laptop and plug it in. But of course, I quickly drape one of Eden's fleece blankets over my sister before going on the hunt; can't let her go cold. Once all of the videos and photos finally load up, I don't hesitate to start madly scrolling through them to find all of the videos I've watched and the images I've viewed. And I end up choosing to click on the last photo that I saw before promising myself I wouldn't touch this drive for the rest of the week, the one with both of them in it... Connie and Austin.

I go back up to the tv again, play it, pause it on the part that his hand appears and where the ring is clearly showing this time, then take out the ring that I purchased.

What. The. Fuck. I bought the same ring, just a different colour.

"No, no, no, no..." I mutter with a breaking voice as I feel tears beginning to well up in my eyes. I know, I should be glad I just uncovered the answer to this mystery, but I'm not. I let this motherfucker near my sister, hold my sister, talk to her for a second, but so are other people making themselves and their children do so. The fact that I even gave this sick fucker a chance, after what Eden told me. I'm fucking livid.

Photo 5

"You don't have class today?" I hear Eden ask.

"I don't feel like going," I answer while rubbing my eyes. I didn't get a second of sleep. But I don't care, and getting rest doesn't matter right now. I'm taking Cheryl home today, then I'm alerting the authorities immediately.

"What's wrong?"

My energy must be off, as always since this flash drive shit started happening. "Can I tell you that later?" I reply, with my head turned towards her, but my eyes, looking in Cheryl's direction. Eden immediately understands and complies.

"Sure."

I'm just waiting on the flash drive I bought, so I could give it to Cheryl, and take her home. She won't know the difference. "Come here." I mouth to her, before opening a window on my laptop.

"You have Aus—..."

"Don't even think about it..." I disrupt her before his damned name even comes flying out of her mouth. I purchased one of his background check reports last night. I found nothing shady, but there will be a court record soon when I'm done with this.

It only shows me nobody has said anything about him yet.

"Why?"

"I'll tell you later."

⊙ ⊙ ⊙ ⊙ ⊙ ⊙

Fuck! Now that I think about it, our parents are going to be pissed when they find out I let Cheryl be around a child molester, and I let him... I feel like a fucking failure! I feel like I failed to protect my sister!

After I drop her off and give her the new flash drive, I start to drive almost past the required speed limit, bawling the entire way home, to immediately get onto the report. And when I get back, and Eden notices how red and puffy my eyes are, she finally discerns this as a serious matter. "What's going on, Bradley?"

"Austin is a rapist."

"Whoa, Bradley! How do you know that? That is a serious claim, that's not something that should be thrown around any kind of way."

"Eden! I have all of the evidence anybody could... hold on." I know she's concerned, and there's a vast difference between a creep and a rapist or pedophile, but I would never make such claims about someone unless I know there's clear evidence of it. This flash drive has everything detectives could ever dream of having while investigating crimes. That's why no faces are showing in any of the photos or videos, he knew one day or another it'd be discovered, but he'd get away with it.

I show her everything the drive consists of, including the videos and photos I've already analyzed. Which again and will always bring me to tears. Then I bring up the video Cheryl fell asleep watching last night and show her everything I caught and led me to this.

"You can report him, Bradley, have a court case, but don't be surprised if they let him go without any consequences."

"What do you mean?"

"Well, think about it. What's one thing you and Austin have in common?"

"I don't know, I don't know this asshole."

"You're both rich, white men. And this justice system is specifically made for rich white people, famous people especially, to succeed without consequences, no matter what crime they committed. Now, what do Connie, your sister, and I have in common?"

"You're girls?"

"Yes, but not just that. I'm black, your sister is biracial, Connie might be black, she has dark skin. Dark skin people are not treated as equals in the system, as you or someone who looks like you would be. Even if the evidence is right in their faces, they don't care. The richer, the less or no consequences. Connie is a dark skin girl, they will most likely not care enough to help her. Won't do shit to him, brush the whole thing off, and sweep it under the rug."

Didn't think about that. "Eden, I'm not brushing this shit under the rug just because a white supremacist system doesn't give a fuck, she's in danger, she needs help, and that motherfucker needs his ass beat and thrown under a prison. It they don't help her, then I will. And at least the world will know who he really is."

"I'm just stating a fact," She sighs, "don't get upset if they deem him innocent even with all the evidence. Be careful."

"3745 Caliphate Ave.," This motherfucker is going down.

The Court Case

"What are you talking about? Genevieve is my little cousin, I would never hurt her."

Lies, lies, fucking lies, and more fucking lies. I know Eden told me not to get upset if they dismiss the evidence and let him go, what she said is still with me, and it doesn't look like it's going to backfire anytime soon. But all of the evidence and the girl, Connie—who's real name is apparently Genevieve—is loud and clear in everybody's fucking face. Her hair is just straightened, and they won't let her talk yet.

Austin knows it's his fucking flash drive, he made the contents of it, his clothes are identical to the man in the pictures, the ring, and now he's lying straight to everybody's face under oath. The scary thing is, people are fucking believing him, despite the photos and videos! The other thing is, she's the same girl who was on her phone I saw at the pop-up shop when I took Cheryl to one of his gigs months ago. So, if anybody else has been to those events, has gone there and paid enough attention, they should be able to recognize her with her straightened hair. "This fucking liar... Jesus Christ," I whisper to myself. My only hope now is Genevieve.

After an interminable, say a good 10 or 15 minutes of lawyers bickering, they finally un-gag (not literally)

Genevieve to let her talk, make her swear under oath, then start asking the questions that really matter.

I hope she knows that I'm only doing this to help her... they can do whatever the fuck they want to him. He deserves every piece of shit thrown at his ass after this.

"Genevieve... Kaiser?"

"Yes."

"You're one of Austin's cousins, correct?"

"Yes."

"Has he ever called you by the name Connie?"

"Ye-" She suddenly hesitates, a terrified look suddenly in her eyes, "yes. A couple of times."

Whoa... busted! Fucking busted!

"Only a couple? Do you know why?"

"Yes. My middle name is Catherine. I don't think he meant to say it."

"Has he ever forced or coerced you to do anything?"

"Not that I can recall."

"Do you recall anything from these photos and videos happening to you?"

"No..."

Fuck! Genevieve... she's terrified of him. That look in her eyes, and I'm sure many others in this room notice it too. And how the fuck do you mix up Catherine with Connie?! No, no, no, no! He scared her into covering his ass!

"Anything you'd like to add?"

"No."

How could I forget that rich and famous people can and usually bribe their victims into keeping quiet and covering for them? "Fuck..." I curse to myself. This entire case is fucked!

⊙ ⊙ ⊙ ⊙ ⊙ ⊙

I hate myself, I hate this case, I hate Austin, and I hate this fucking world! But Eden told me, I can't get upset. But I'm not upset, I'm fucking fuming.

The only way they would need or even want to reopen this case is if other people come out about him, which is very unlikely to happen now. Genevieve won't let up; what will make others want to? And they probably wouldn't take Eden and her experience with him seriously since she's my girlfriend. I hate this, I'm such a fucking failure!

To keep myself alert and calm instead of giving the mirror in front of me an enraged smash with one of my hands, I splash my face with cold water. Eden's waiting for me.

As soon as I gather myself back together and muster up my confidence to walk out, I turn around to see this motherfucking liar, rapist, pedophile, goof, you name it, Austin, standing the right amount of feet away from me, glaring. I throw a weak glare back, before immediately smarting off, "What the fuck do you want?" One thing I never saw coming. He suddenly takes me into a chokehold with both of his hands clasped around my neck, making me bang my back and the back of my head against the nearest wall.

"Your girl Eden is pretty." He snarls into my ear, "She's next... if you don't stay out of my fucking business and leave Connie alone."

He finally releases his grip on my neck. And as I'm gasping for air after nearly suffocating, he quickly fixes himself like the fucking jackass he is, and like nothing happened, then leaves me alone in the bathroom.

Still in shock, I leave the bathroom, find Eden, and begin to sob into one of her shoulders like the real fucking failure I am, while I watch this good for nothing asshole walk further and further down the hall, away with Connie.

Acknowledgements

For those of you who finished this, thank you,
and I wish this story was just an idea.

Christina, Charlie, Emily, I love you.